Willie Nelson Bi[o]
The Legendary Outl[aw]

"Ninety-nine percent of the world's lovers are not with their first choice. That's what makes the jukebox play."

- Willie Nelson -

By Chris Michael Hoyt

Copyright © 2023 by Chris Michael Hoyt
All rights reserved.

The content of this book may not be reproduced, duplicated, or transmitted without the author's or publisher's express written permission. Under no circumstances will the publisher or author be held liable or legally responsible for any damages, reparation, or monetary loss caused by the information contained in this book, whether directly or indirectly.

Legal Notice:
This publication is copyrighted. It is strictly for personal use only. You may not change, distribute, sell, use, quote, or paraphrase any part of this book without the author's or publisher's permission.

Disclaimer Notice:
Please keep in mind that the information in this document is only for educational and entertainment purposes. Every effort has been made to present accurate, up-to-date, reliable, and comprehensive information. There are no express or implied warranties. Readers understand that the author is not providing legal, financial, medical, or professional advice. This book's content was compiled from a variety of sources. Please seek the advice of a licensed professional before attempting any of the techniques described in this book. By reading this document, the reader agrees that the author is not liable for any direct or indirect losses incurred as a result of using the information contained within this document, including, but not limited to, errors, omissions, or inaccuracies.

TABLE OF CONTENTS

INTRODUCTION

A native of Texas

Following High School

The City Of Fort Worth

Houston

Nashville

"Hello Walls."

Having Fun With Ray Price

Making a Record of His Own Work

Trigger

Reunion in Dripping Springs

Stranger with a Red Head

The Big Deal

"To All the Girls I've Ever Known"

The Roadrunners

Farm Assistance

Tax Issues

Missouri, Branson

The Twentieth Century

Willie Nelson's Legacy

Afterword

CONCLUSION

INTRODUCTION

In 2000, I married for the second time, and my bride and I spent our honeymoon in Las Vegas. I scoured the internet for concerts performing in Vegas at the time, and we chose three to watch. Among them was

Willie Nelson is a musician. He was performing at a little club just off the strip, so the audience was limited. We sat just a few feet away from Willie and watched him sing and perform his show. What a great evening.

Now, one of the other acts we saw in Vegas was David Copperfield, and while he was wonderful and we enjoyed the illusions he performed, Willie is what I remember about going to Las Vegas sixteen years later.

Willie Nelson is to country music what apple pie and baseball are to America. Willie Nelson is the unique performer who appeals to people of all musical inclinations.

It doesn't imply everyone likes Willie, but I doubt you'd be reading this book if you didn't. He has had an incredible career over the years. Willie has always been a loner. He does what he wants without regard for the repercussions. I can't tell you how much I've enjoyed telling the tale of Willie Nelson's life and music. I hope you enjoy it.

A native of Texas

Willie Hugh Nelson was born on April 29, 1933, in Abbott, Texas. He was born just before midnight on the 29th, but when the doctor filled out the birth certificate, he noted that he was born on the 30th. If you go to imdb.com, they still state Willie's birthday is April 30, when it was actually April 29. From the moment he was born, he had flaming red hair. Willie's older sister, Bobbie Lee, died before him in 1931.

Abbott, Texas had a population of 326 people in 1930, making it a small town. It is approximately 70 miles south of Dallas and 26 miles north of Waco, Texas. I recently drove from Dallas to Austin on I-35. I drove within a few miles of Willie Nelson's birthplace and had no idea. Willie describes Abbott as a "no-horse" town (as opposed to a "one-horse town") since the sole horse that lived anywhere near them was two miles out of town, just over the city limit.

The year was 1933, and the country was under the grip of the Great Depression. Willie's mother was Myrle Marie Nelson (maiden name: Greenshaw), and his father was mechanic Ira Doyle Nelson. There's not much to say about Willie's parents because they both abandoned him when he was young and were never a part of his life. Myrle left the family soon after Willie was born, and without a wife, Ira followed. Ira stayed in Abbott for a while but left Willie's upbringing to his grandparents, Alfred and Nancy Nelson, or Mama Nelson and Papa Nelson, as Willie called them.

Willie was raised by his grandparents from then on, and he saw little of his own father and mother. Ira eventually divorced Myrle and remarried, and Willie only saw him every now and again during his childhood. His parents didn't even give him a name. Mildred, one of his cousins, gave him his name. Hugh was also his middle name, which she gave him. Haughty was his nickname throughout his childhood.

Mom and Papa Nelson were both music fans. Mother taught music to local children who were interested. Papa could play the guitar, and Willie did as well.

When Willie was six, he bought an inexpensive one from Sears to teach him how to play. Mama Nelson began teaching Bobbie to play the piano on an old pump-organ they possessed. Bobbie created a cardboard piano to practice her fingering until they could afford to buy an actual piano. Bobbie rose to prominence as a gifted pianist. She's been with Willie's band since the beginning.

Music had always been a part of their family, but things changed when Mama and Papa Nelson purchased a new Philco radio. They may now listen to American music. While they were in Texas, you can guess that the majority of the music they heard was country. In the 1930s, country music was barely getting begun. Willie listened to musicians such as Jimmie Rodgers and The Carter Family. Individuals like this sowed the seed that would blossom into Willie Nelson, an adult country artist. Willie was also a fan of Ernest Tubb and Bob Wills. Ernest Tubb was his first singing idol, he adds.

Alfred or Papa Nelson died abruptly in 1940, when Willie was six years old, as a result of pneumonia complications. He was 56 years old. Willie wasn't old enough to grasp what death was all about, but he knew he was now the man of the house, and if things weren't already difficult, they became much more difficult once Papa died.

Willie discovered that he excelled at penning simple poems. His grandfather's death appeared to kick him into overdrive, as he found himself writing more and more about grief and alienation. Even at the age of seven, he had a mature outlook on life. The family had previously lived on a farm with animals, but with Grandpa gone, they were forced to leave and go to town, where Mama Nelson struggled to make ends meet for the two children.

Willie started writing music and playing in bands by the age of ten. He had to pick cotton in the fall because that's what everyone did to make a living. He soon discovered, though, that he could earn just as much or more by performing in a local family band.

Willie improved steadily throughout his adolescence. He had an entire book of songs composed by the time he was thirteen. He discovered, much to his grandmother's chagrin, that the money was made in the bars and salons. So, despite Mama Nelson's displeasure, that's where he ended up.

went. Nobody seemed to care that he was underage. He drank and became inebriated with the rest of the guys. Willie claims he knew he was heading to hell since he was a child, so why not have some fun along the way? Bobbie married a soldier who had recently returned from the war. It was the summer between Bobbie's junior and senior years in high school in 1947.

Bobbie was sixteen years old, Willie was fourteen, and the soldier she married was named Bud Fletcher. This made quite a stir in the small town of Abbott, Texas. Bobbie had one more year of high school left, and married females simply did not return to school. Bobbie, on the other hand, did. She wanted her diploma, so she returned and completed her senior year, graduating. Fletcher formed Bud Fletcher and the Texans, a band modeled after Bob Wills and the Texas Playboys. Willie was on lead guitar, while Bobbie was on keyboard. Interestingly, their father, Ira, played guitar and occasionally fiddled in the band. Although Ira did not play an active role in their lives, he was presumably around from time to time.

Willie remained with the Texans through high school. He even had a fan club composed of three or four of his classmates. That looks like a terrific strategy to get through high school to me. He graduated in 1950, which would not be so impressive if just approximately 11% of the population of his area (Hill County) had completed high school. So Willie was part of a select group. Bobbie had also graduated. Mama Nelson was overjoyed.

Following High School

High school had come to an end. What should I do now? Willie had no idea what he wanted to do. He spent most of his time with pals drinking and waking up drunk. He didn't have any work, and while he wanted to join a band, nothing came up. He and a pal found work pruning trees one day. That appeared to be honest work until Willie fell out of a tree he was cutting and injured his back. He'd experience back pain for the rest of his life.

Therefore, once again out of job, he felt that the only option was to join the AirForce. He was of draftable age and knew they'd come after him at some point, so why not enlist and get it over with? He didn't have anything else to do. It was 1950, and he hadn't even graduated from high school for a full year. So he joined the Air Force. He was assigned to Lackland AFB in San Antonio, Texas, and then to Sheppard AFB in Wichita Falls, Texas, Scott AFB in Illinois, and Keesler AFB in Biloxi, Mississippi. Now, I find that very fascinating because, in 1960, I was also stationed at Lackland AFB for Basic Training, which was not exceptional because everyone who joined the Air Force went there. But from there, I transferred to Keesler AFB in Biloxi. Therefore, ten years after Willie, I served at the same bases he did. I feel much more connected to him now.

As he joined the army, he brought his guitar with him. Bud Fletcher and the Texans were playing in a nearby town while he was at Sheppard AFB, so he got to sit in with them on weekends and whenever he could get away.

Willie was only in the Air Force for about nine months. Getting drunk every weekend didn't help, and he developed a reputation for getting into fights on a regular basis, but it was his back that eventually allowed him to be discharged. The fall from the tree a few years before had caused permanent harm, and it had begun to annoy him greatly. Instead of tarnishing his record, he was given an honorable medical release. He committed not to sue the military for back problems that they had not caused.

Willie was so liberated and ready to return home. Yet things had changed dramatically at home. He attempted to rejoin Bud Fletcher's group, but it was disbanded. Bud Fletcher had a nasty temper, and the band had tolerated it for as long as they could, therefore the Texans were no longer. Willie Nelson Fan Club, composed of girls from his high school class, had gone their separate ways. Willie was lonely in Abbott since his father, Ira, had relocated to Dallas. He just had one remaining friend. Willie had met Zeke Varnon, an old acquaintance of Bud Fletcher, right out of high school. He reconnected with Zeke, and the two of them traveled to Waco to see what the big city had to offer.

His first wife was the major thing he gained from Waco. He met Martha Jewel Matthews in a drive-in, one of those places where the carhops ride around on roller shakes. But Martha didn't do it. Willie was instantly smitten by Martha, a gorgeous brunette with long hair, and eventually won her heart. On October 27, 1952, they married, and he moved her to Abbott to live with Mama Nelson.

Lana, their first daughter, was born in Abbott on November 11, 1955, but Willie realized straight away that he couldn't sustain a family there, so he returned to Waco to find employment. However, on May 11, a massive tornado had hit Waco, and it was not in the mood to create much work. Willie stayed in town for a year or so while attending Baylor University while the town was still healing from the disaster. Willie was officially studying agriculture, but he had considered law. He was paying for his education through the G.I. Bill, but that didn't last long because he only served nine months. University life was simply not for him, and he soon found himself yearning for another place to be. Therefore, in 1954, Willie left Waco for San Antonio, bringing his wife and child with him.

Willie looked for a band to play with in San Antonio (he really lived in Pleasanton, which was about 6 miles south of San Antonio). He discovered one at the Mission City Playboys. Johnny Bush, who rapidly became friends with Willie, ran it. They performed at every club in and around San Antonio. They even made it to Houston every now and then. On one such journey to Houston in 1955, they recorded a few songs onto tape to take back to San Antonio and have them made onto 45 rpm records at a local record company called Sarg Records. "The Storm" was one of the tunes.

The songs "Has Just Started" and "After I've Sang My Last Hillbilly Song" were hoped to be played on the radio. Sarg Records was said to have rejected the music online, although this was not the case. It simply ignored them. Willie didn't hear anything.

Martha couldn't handle the fact that Willie was in a band. For one thing, it did not generate enough revenue to maintain them. As a result, Willie secured a real job as a disc jockey at a local radio station, KBOP-AM. Sure, he said the management, he had a lot of experience as a DJ. That, of course, was a lie. Yet he was rather skilled at it. He went from radio station to radio station, trying to make a life. Yet this irritated Martha even more. She wanted him to come home and to work. He reasoned that if we went to Fort Worth, I might be able to do both.

The City Of Fort Worth

His father, Ira, had relocated to Fort Worth to assist Willie in finding a job. In the mid-1950s, Fort Worth, Texas, was truly the Wild West. When you played at a Fort Worth pub or club, there was chicken wire stretched up between the band and the customers to keep the band members safe from hurled bottles. Willie enjoyed it. He was in a few bands and worked at a few radio stations. He worked for KCNC in Fort Worth, and he would sing along to the tunes that were aired on the radio. Even when he was reading advertising, he would sing along with them and strum his guitar. Everyone was soon listening to Willie Nelson on the radio. The station was impressed, so they offered him a half-hour show called The Wectern Exprecc in the early afternoon, where he would sing lullabies to children who were listening so they could sleep. "The Red-Headed Stranger," a song he performed to the children, was written in the 1950s by Edith Linderman and Carl Stutz. The song was written for Perry Como, but he never recorded it. Willie chose it for his radio show and eventually recorded it as the title song for an album in 1974.

Fort Worth was a crazy town with plenty of venues to play and hone your art, but none of it paid anything. When you played at a bar, more often than not, the proprietor would tell you at the end of the night that there was no money to pay you. Willie thus played but produced little. Martha got a job as a waitress, which paid more than Willie did. He continued to write songs and play whenever he could, but nothing was happening. Even though he didn't see his mother, Myrle, very often, she did visit her grandchildren on occasion. Willie was summoned to the Northwest by Myrle. There was work to be done. Willie decided to fly to Eugene, Oregon, to investigate what was going on and if he could make a livelihood there.

So he, Martha, and Lana packed their belongings and relocated to Portland, Oregon. It doesn't imply he went straight there. He'd heard that San Diego, California was an excellent area to play country music, so they pulled over and Willie looked for work. Yet, you couldn't work in San Diego unless you were a union member, and you couldn't become a union member.

unless you had the money to get in, and Willie and family had no money, so they kept walking till they were at Portland. In the meantime, Mother Myrle had relocated to Portland from Eugene, so they had a place to stay.

Willie began his career in Portland by doing what he had done in Texas: he got a job working at a local radio station. This time, KVAN 910 was on the line. His show was called, you guessed it, "The Western Express," and he could have stayed in Texas since everything was the same in Portland. The only change was that Willie did not sing along with the tunes this time. He simply pretended to be a disc jockey and played music. He was popular at the station.

Willie's decision to go to Portland was one of the best things he accomplished during this period. In Texas, being a cowboy was commonplace; everyone was a cowboy. In Portland, being a cowboy was a huge deal; he stood out from the crowd. He wandered around town in buckskins and with two handguns on his hip (both plugged). He quickly became a local celebrity, and the money began to flow in. He saved up enough money to buy a bright red Cadillac convertible to drive about town in luxury. If he hadn't already been spotted, he was now.

In the Portland/Vancouver area, "The Western Express" became immensely popular. He began with an hour-long show and quickly expanded to three hours. He rose to the status of local fame. As a result, he took advantage of the situation and used the radio station's equipment to make a 45 rpm record. He called Starday Records in Texas and provided them with a tape of the song, "No Place For Me." Willie got his first record when they made 500 copies.

Paul, Martha, and Lana relocated to Vancouver, Washington, just across the Columbia River from Portland, and soon after, another daughter joined their family. Susie Nelson was born on the 20th of January, 1957. With two children and both Martha and Willie working, they needed some assistance, so Martha's parents relocated to Vancouver to assist.

Even though he was making decent money in Portland, he wasn't planning on staying long. He didn't want to spend the rest of his life as a disc jockey. He was a lyricist who aspired to play the guitar. He kept writing in the hopes that something would happen. It happened one day.

Mae Boren Axton arrived in town. I doubt you've heard of her, but she was known as the "Queen Mother of Nashville" in the 1950s. Her biggest claim to fame was co-writing the smash hit "Heartbreak Hotel," which Elvis Presley took to number one on both the pop and country charts, launching the career of the most famous rock singer in history, Elvis Presley. So Mae Axton wielded power. Willie persuaded her to sit down and listen to a few of his tunes. He had recordings of the tunes, and she listened to them all. She informed Willie that he shouldn't be in Oregon, but rather in Nashville or, at the very least, Texas. He needed to be in the thick of things.

She informed him that if he came east, she would do everything she could to help him. She also told him she'd be a very happy woman if she could write half as good as Willie. Willie was overjoyed. A few weeks later, radio station KVAN shifted its format from country to rock-and-roll and began playing songs by that newcomer, Elvis Presley. Willie saw the writing on the wall and planned to depart Oregon for Fort Worth.

Willie wasn't interested in Nashville at the moment, but he would be in the future. He needed to be close to family and friends right now, and Fort Worth seemed more like home. So he and his family returned to Fort Worth. Willie stopped in Springfield, Missouri, on his way home, to see an old buddy, Billy Walker, perform. He and Walker had both worked at the same Waco radio station, and Walker had cut a few records, some of which charted. Willie showed Billy

Walker some of his compositions, and on April 28, 1959, Billy Walker recorded his first Willie Nelson original. Willie had composed "The Storm Within My Heart" as a child years before, but the song had never been recorded. Walker's "The Storm Within My Heart" was not a hit, although it did garner rotation on Texas radio stations.

On May 21, 1958, Martha gave birth to their third child and first son, William Hugh Nelson Jr (they called him Billy). Fort Worth was still Fort Worth; nothing had changed since he departed. Willie was still having difficulty finding work and getting people to listen to him. He and Martha were soon out of money, and he was forced to sell the Cadillac. He bought a used car that got them around but wasn't as flashy.

Willie had odd jobs to put food on the table and worked as much as he could in pubs and clubs. He was only waiting to be found. While waiting, he worked in a granary, laying carpet, selling encyclopedias over the phone, and working at a service station. Willie didn't last long in any job because he was often dismissed. Because he was out every night playing somewhere or writing poems, the boss would find him sleeping (which were really lyrics to songs.)

There was the Louisiana Hayride and the Big D Jamboree in Dallas, as well as the Grand Ole Opry in Nashville (which still exists to some extent). These were all heard on the radio. Willie ultimately got a spot in the band for the Cowtown Hoedown, which was also held in Fort Worth. Uncle Hank Craig ran the Hoedown, and Craig ran a local record label named D Records. He liked Willie and his songs, so he signed him to D Records to cut a record. He recorded one single for D Records, "Man With the Blues," while in Waco before moving to Houston.

Houston

Willie had heard nice things about Houston, so he left Martha and the kids in Waco and went to see what he could see. Starday Records, one of Texas' largest record labels, was based in Houston. Gold Star Records, owned by Bill Quinn, was also located in East Houston. Willie wanted to move to Houston since it was the headquarters of D Records. George Jones recorded several of his early records for them, as did other notables like The Big Bopper (remember "Chantilly Lace?"). He reasoned that because he had previously recorded one track for them, being closer to the firm would offer him an advantage on future recordings. And he was correct. They quickly arranged for him to record his second single for D Records, "What a Way to Live," which was released in May 1960. Bill Quinn produced the album, which was recorded at Gold Star Studios.

Willie had taken all of the songs he had written over the previous few years with him. Willie was ready to sell tunes like "Family Bible," "Mr Record Man," "Crazy," and "Funny How Time Slips Away" to anyone who would buy them. It takes time to become famous in the music industry, and Willie felt he would make it someday. Yet, he needed to eat and support his family right now. Willie needed to obtain a job while the record industry was in motion.

He approached Larry Butler, sang some of his songs for him, and was hired to play in his band. They performed at the Esquire Ballroom in Houston, and because he was now working steadily, Willie returned to Waco and relocated his family to the Houston region. He had a day job at radio station KRCT in Pasadena, Texas, a Houston suburb, so he relocated his family to Pasadena. Willie drove thirty miles from his house to the Esquire Ballroom every day. He was writing songs in his brain while driving. He was unconcerned about remembering them. He was confident he could. Many outstanding songs were written throughout those years. "Night Life" was one of the greatest.

D Records' Pappy Daily declined to record "Night Life" because he didn't think it was country enough. Willie sold the song to Pete Buskirk, a guitar instructor, for $150, and Buskirk recorded it for a small local label called Rx Records (medication for happier times). Willie still sang on the record, but the artist was credited as Pete Buskirk and the Little Men with Hugh Nelson. Of course, the single failed to chart, but it was heard, and as Willie grew in popularity, other artists began to cover the song.

The label renamed the song "Nite Life" so they wouldn't get in trouble for recording a tune they didn't own. Ray Price purchased and recorded the song in 1960. It was a success for him, peaking at number 28 on the nation charts. Price chats to the audience on the first track of his album Nightlife and introduces the album in general, but he adds the first song, "Night Life," was written particularly for him by a lad down Texas way. That was not true, but no one realized it at the time. "Night Life" developed its own personality. It was recorded by a wide range of artists, including Frank Sinatra, B.B. King, and David Lee Roth. It is now considered a classic. Willie eventually got to record the song himself, and he and Danny Davis charted it at number twenty in 1980.

Willie continued to write tunes. He sold "Family Bible" to a new vocalist named Claude Gray, and it charted at number 10 for him. This aided Gray as well as Willie. Willie recorded his first hit. He hadn't sung it, and his name wasn't on the record label stating that he wrote it, but industry insiders knew he had. His name was being mentioned all across the country. It was time to move on from Houston and into the big leagues. It was finally time to travel to Nashville.

So, leaving Martha and the kids in Houston, he hopped in his beat-up old automobile and drove north toward Nashville, Tennessee, the country music capital.

Nashville

Willie moved to Nashville in 1960, while I joined the Air Force. Only one of them is historically significant. I endured basic training in Texas before being assigned to Biloxi, Mississippi, for the remainder of my four-year deployment. Listening to the radio was one of the things I remember most about that time in my life. In the barracks, I had a little tube-model that didn't pick up much but local stations, but I also had a car. I could drive down to my car after dark and listen to the radio. I picked up stations all across the south from that automobile. Practically every 50,000-watt, clear channel station could be picked up, including WSM in Nashville. I sat in that old Plymouth sedan several nights, just listening.

WSM is a country music station. They performed at the Grand Ole Opry, which originated at the Ryman Auditorium, and in the early 1960s, you could hear artists such as Ernest Tubb, Dottie West, Roy Acuff, and many others. WSM and the Grand Ole Opry were Willie's goals.

He hadn't been in town more than a week when he ran into an old acquaintance from Fort Worth, Billy Walker. Walker wasn't a big name at the time; he was still looking for his big "breakthrough," but he knew a lot more than Willie and had contacts. He also realized that success and recognition did not always come easily, so he hired Willie to sell encyclopedias door-to-door (for approximately a day) and let him live with him and his wife. He even had Willie send for the rest of the family, so Martha and her three children boarded a Greyhound bus bound for Nashville to join Willie. They all spent some time at Billy Walker's place.
Willie attempted to market his music, but no one was interested. He hung around with Walker until they stumbled to Tootsie's Orchid Lounge, a dingy club frequented by many of Nashville's songwriters. Willy immediately felt at ease. There he met Hank Cochran, an aspiring writer who would have a lackluster singing career over the next twenty years or so. He did, however, know how to write tunes. Cochran penned many terrific songs throughout the years, but his

first big hit was "I Fall To Pieces," which Patsy Cline sang and made a number one country record.

Willie finally got Martha and the kids a more habitable apartment. He rented a trailer in Dunn's Trailer Park for the entire family to live in. Martha obtained a job as a waitress, and even though money was tight, they made it. Willie brought Hank Cochran home to the trailer one night, and Hank chuckled and said it was the very trailer he and his family had lived in when they first arrived in Nashville. To top it off, Hank told Willie that Roger Miller and his family had lived in the same trailer when they relocated to Nashville. That is one well-known trailer. A sign that reads "Trailers For Sale or Rent" hangs over the entrance to Dunn's Trailer Park. Do you recall it from Roger Miller's song "King of the Road?" "

"Hello Walls."

Willie met Faron Young through Hank Cochran and pitched him the song "Hello Walls" (among others). Faron was impressed and wanted to record the tune. Willie told Faron that he wanted $500 for "Hello Walls," but Faron, perhaps sensing the quality of the song he was purchasing, told Willie that he wouldn't buy it, but he would loan Willie $500 for the time being, and Willie would retain ownership of the song and receive a cut of the profits from sales.

"Hello Walls" debuted at number one on the country chart and remained there for two weeks. It also made it to the pop chart, where it peaked at number twelve. Faron Young had only one song on the pop chart. Willie received his first royalty cheque for $14,000. You can figure out how many copies of the single were sold if you remember that each single sold rewarded the writer of the song exactly one cent. Of course, this was only the first royalty payment. "Hello Walls" would sell for years, and many other artists would cover it. Today, it is regarded as a country music classic. He's lucky he didn't sell the song to Young. Nevertheless, while the money was significant and helped Willie pay his expenses, the most important aspect was that Willie Nelson had become a household celebrity in Nashville. "Hello Walls" would open up a lot of possibilities.

Willie was on a roll, or was about to start one. Hank Cochran, who had sold Patsy Cline's song "I Fall to Pieces," approached her husband, Charlie Dick, and played Willie's song "Crazy." Dick was hooked, but Patsy didn't like Willie and refused to record the song. It didn't take long for Dick to persuade his wife to record it. And she did it. She did all of the vocals in one take. The rest of it, the background singers, who were, by the way, Jordanaires, took a little longer. We are all aware of what occurred. The song went on to become one of Patsy Cline's biggest hits. It stayed at number two on the country chart for two weeks and eventually became one of Patsy's hallmark songs.

"Crazy," like "Hello Walls," made it to the pop charts and peaked at number nine. This meant a lot of money for Willie as a pop chart song.

Having Fun With Ray Price

Willie wanted to play and be a member of a band more than he wanted to write songs. It all changed when Ray Price called and asked if he could play bass (Willie replied yes even though he couldn't) and if he wanted to tour with him and his band. Ray Price's bassist has left the band to pursue other interests. That guy was Donald Lytle, who eventually changed his name to Johnny Paycheck ("Take This Job and Shove It"). Thus, on the way to their first gig, Willie learned how to play the bass and briefly joined Ray Prices' band.

Willie only stayed with Price for a short time, but it was enough to ruin his marriage. Willie couldn't get enough of the road babes who followed the band wherever they went. As the band concluded, the females would wait offstage, and what was a man to do? You were expected to bring one back to the motel.

The womanizing ultimately caught up with Martha, and she realized their relationship was over. I believe it all came to a head one night when Martha and Willie were staying at a motel and a woman called asking for Willie. When Martha responded, she heard a woman ask when she and Willie were going to meet. She had no idea she was conversing with Willie's wife. When Willie entered the room, Martha held a whiskey bottle to his head, and it took two police officers to break them up. Because Martha was the one who assaulted Willie, she was detained and spent a few hours in jail before Willie was able to get her released.

That effectively ended their marriage. In 1960, they divorced. Martha brought the children to Las Vegas, where she filed for divorce. Before I leave Martha, there's one more story I'd like to tell you. I believe every Willie Nelson fan is aware of this story, but it deserves to be memorialized here. There was a rumor that Willie came home intoxicated one night, passed out on the bed, and Martha sewed a bed sheet around him so he couldn't escape and then beat him with a broomstick. That is just half correct. That wasn't a sheet, but rather two jump ropes belonging to her children. She placed them beneath Willie's body and fastened them tight, preventing him from moving. She then beat him with a broomstick. It was retaliation for all of his womanizing.

Willie didn't have to look far to find another woman. He was already involved with Shirley Collie, despite the fact that she was also married. Willie, on the other hand, knew he was in love the moment he saw her, so he wasn't concerned that they'd end up together.

Making a Record of His Own Work

Willie's decision to relocate to Nashville proved wise, as he immediately secured a recording contract with Liberty Records. His debut single, "The Part When I Cry," was recorded in Los Angeles. Willie, as a relative unknown in the realm of country music, did not sell many recordings. The single simply faded out and died. Willie, on the other hand, was unconcerned. He now had confirmation that he could sing. He realized the money was in live appearances, so he used the record as a bargaining chip to secure performing dates. On the other hand, "Mr. Record Man" was played on the radio more than the A-side, and his name became well-known. The record only sold 4000 copies, the most of which were in Texas, but it was enough to spur a sequel.

He requested Shirley Collie to sing with him on his second attempt. She'd been in the business for a while and understood what she was doing. Shirley Angelina Simpson was born in 1921 in Chillicothe, Missouri. She began singing as a teenager and had at least three singles on Liberty before joining Willie. Her first husband was Biff Collie, a well-known country disc jockey in Texas. They married in 1958, but it didn't last long once she met Willie. They were divorced by the 196s, and she married Willie.

The second song was a duet by Willie and Shirley called "Willingly," which charted at number ten on the country chart. Willie's debut appearance on the chart. Interestingly, Willie did not write this song; instead, his friend Hank Cochran did. But Cochran must have known the Willie and Shirley story since it absolutely describes them. The song is about their relationship and how they "willingly" fell in love despite the fact that they both belonged to someone else. Willie's voice is not suitable for duets. Many artists did not want to sing with him, but Shirley's voice blended perfectly with Willie's, and they had great success.

He followed "Willingly" with "Touch Me," which he wrote. "Touch Me" peaked at number seven on the country charts, but Willie couldn't keep it up. It was released in 1962, and it took thirteen years (until 1975) for Willie to return to the top ten. His career could have ended even before it began.

Willie wanted to create an album, and Liberty Records consented because he had three singles under his belt, so he recorded and released...And Then I Wrote, his first album, in September 1962. Many of the songs on the CD were written by Willie Nelson but made famous by other singers. Among his songs are "Crazy," "Hello Walls," and "Strange How Time Slips By." "Touch Me," his highest charting song to date, is on the album, but "Willingly" isn't; there doesn't appear to be any record that the song is on any album; it appears to exist solely as a single. And then I wrote that it did not sell and did not chart.

Willie formed his own band, which included Shirley Collie on vocals and bass. They moved around, playing wherever they could find work. Willie and Shirley secured a room at the Golden Nugget in Las Vegas and decided to marry while they were there. Willie and Shirley married on January 12, 1996, at the Chapel of Love in Las Vegas. He wasn't entirely separated from Martha at this point, and he wouldn't be for several months. Willie was technically married to two ladies for a few months. Yet no one cared. At the time, it didn't seem like a huge problem.

Here'c Willie Nelson, his second album on the Liberty label, too failed to chart. It had one hit single, "Half a Man," which peaked at number 25 on the singles list.

Willie was notorious among musicians of the time for being tough to play with. To make the song sound correct, you have to be familiar with his style. Willie always sang behind the rhythm, making it difficult for the musicians to keep up with him. Someone told him he'd make a terrific jazz singer, and he even recorded a jazz standard, "Am I Blue," and he did a fantastic job of it. But I'm pleased he didn't try jazz. Country would have lost a legend.

Willie was already in difficulty with the IRS by the 196s, a situation that would haunt him for the rest of his life. He was simply too busy and broke to think about something as insignificant as paying taxes. As a result, the IRS began to congregate around the locations where he performed, and when he exited the stage, they waited for him. Willie's taxes were paid when the venue accountant handed him a check for that night's concert and the IRS agent relieved him of it.

Willie and Shirley closed on a house in Ridgetop, Tennessee, about ten miles north of Nashville, on November 22, 1966, and made plans to move in. This was the day President John F. Kennedy was assassinated in Dallas, Texas. Willie was relieved to be free of Texas. They'd both been on the road for years and needed a rest. They decided to settle in for a while and unwind. Shirley, it turns out, enjoyed being a housewife. She enjoyed cooking, cleaning, and all the other tasks that come with running a household. Willie spent the most of his time creating new songs. Willie's contract with Liberty Records had expired, so he signed with RCA Records and stayed with them for several years.

Shirley stayed at home during the first four years or so they resided in Ridgetop, while Willie traveled with his band. Willie's three children were relocated to Tennessee to live with their father because Willie's first wife Martha perceived a stable living arrangement. The kids enjoyed it as well. Shirley also adored being a stepmother. Everything appeared to be fine, except that Willie still liked to go into town and get drunk while he was at home. He'd come home so drunk that he wouldn't know Shirley. She became tired of it and eventually began messing about while Willie was driving.

RCA continued to release records of Willie's work throughout his four years on the farm in Tennessee, but nothing charted well. He managed to crack the Top 20 twice. "One in a Row" was number nineteen in 1966. Later, in 1968, "Bring Me Sunshine" reached number thirteen. It confirmed Willie's financial potential for the record business, but that was about it. That was the best Willie could do until many years later, in 1975, when he scored number one with "Blue Eyes Crying in the Rain," which we shall discuss later.

Willie went to see Fred Foster, a record producer of Monument Records, in October 1964. About this time, Willie had a brief connection with Monument. Willie had a Christmas song to sell to Foster, but understanding that October was probably too late to record a Christmas song, Willie suggested that they set it up for the next year. Foster was taken aback when he heard the music. He shouted out, "No, it's not too late!"

Monument Records' top singer at the time was based in London, UK. Roy Orbison was that man. The song was "Beautiful Paper," and Orbison swiftly recorded it and published it in time for the 1964 Christmas season. The song peaked at number fifteen on the Billboard Hot 100. Willie Nelson also recorded it that year, but no one knew who he was, and the song did not chart. But, Roy Orbison has made it a classic.

Willie was done with Monument before the end of the year and back with RCA Records. Willie Nelson recorded his version of "Pretty Paper" for RCA. Willie was selected to join the Grand Ole Opry in 1964, owing primarily to his writing of "Crazy" and "Hello Walls," rather than any songs he recorded. The Opry had a reputation as the place to be back then, but it wasn't quite as important as it is now. Willie was honored to be a member of the Opry, but quickly discovered that he would be required to perform every other Friday, Saturday, and Sunday night. Back then, you had to perform at the Opry 26 weekends a year, which was simply too much for Willie. Willie claims that the Opry paid nothing and that he was losing money by performing there when he could be making real money in Texas.

So he dropped out after a year. He departed the Opry and didn't return for several years. Yet once a member, always a member, and Willie's name is still on the roster of Opry members today.

Willie enjoyed the latter half of the Sixties decade, although it didn't pay well. It's a wonder RCA kept him on. In 1965, he released Country Willie - Hic Own Congc, which reached number fourteen on the album chart but did not make him a star because no singles were released from the album. Willie pushed on, undeterred. Country Favorites - Willie Nelson Style, released by RCA in 1966, fared slightly better, peaking at number nine on the album chart. It, however, did not release any singles. These albums have been heard by me. They have a lot of fantastic music on them. Willie has a wonderful voice and some of the best writing in country music. It's unfortunate that he didn't fare well in his early years.

Willie is well-known for his marijuana use. He had attempted it briefly in high school, but by 1965, he had abandoned the practice. According to legend, Willie was offered a joint by a bandmate sometime in 1965 and said, "Nah, I don't smoke that stuff, man." Willie couldn't help but join in when the rest of the band started using it less than a year later. They only acquired high-quality cannabis because they worked regularly.

Willie was playing with Ernest Tubb and the Texas Troubadours during this time period, and they played on the majority of the tracks on these recordings. Willie returned Faron Young's $500 debt to record "Hello Walls" plus interest in 1965. Willie had a $50,000 bull on his Ridgetop farm and had it brought to Faron Young's ranch one day with a note attached that said, "No Bull, Paid in Full." I believe Young got the better of that bargain.

His fourth album was released in May of 1967. Make Way For Willie peaked at number seven, indicating that Willie was doing better. In Nashville, he was dubbed a "little celebrity." He was having an effect, but it wasn't a significant one. This album yielded a single, "One in a Row" (#19), indicating that things were looking up. In 1967, The Party's Over and Other Fabulous Willie Nelson Congc (#9) was released. "The Party's Over," the title track, was written by Willie in the mid 1950s. The song was released as a single from the album and peaked at number 24 on the country chart.

This triumph was followed by another single, "Blackjack County Chain," which was not included on any album. Red Lane wrote this song and originally offered it to Charlie Pride. Pride was only starting out in country music in 1967, but he rejected the song because of the subject nature. The song recounts the assassination of a Georgia sheriff by members of a black chain gang. One of the chain gang members tells the story. This was quite contentious in 1966, and because Charlie Pride is black, he felt it was inappropriate for him to sing the song. Willie, on the other hand, didn't mind singing it and decided to release it as a single. The song peaked at number 21 before being taken from rotation due to concerns over the explicit nature of the lyrics.

One nice thing that came out of "Blackjack County Chain" was that Willie got to know Charlie Pride. He was the first black guy to perform country music, and he may be the topic of a future Legends of Country Music book, but he was largely obscure in 1967. As a result, Willie invited him to join his band. Some were initially opposed to having a black man on stage. After all, it was the late 1960s, and segregation was on everyone's mind. Some people booed when Charlie entered the stage, but once he started singing, everyone adored him. Charlie was so good that it only took a few months for him to outsell Willie in record stores. He eventually abandoned Willie and moved off on his own.

Johnny Bush was another member of Willie's band who had enough expertise playing with Willie to branch out and record his own records. He was never the superstar he may have been, yet he constantly charted from 1967 through 1981. He only ever reached number seven with a song called "You Gave Me a Mountain."

Willie was more concerned in relationships than in getting money, but he was good at both. He would hire people for his band knowing that they were better than average and that it was only a matter of time before they left for something better. That was fine. Willie made new acquaintances everywhere he went.

Trigger

On the road, musicians go through a lot of instruments. Guitar firms were always sending Willie guitars to try out in the hopes of getting an endorsement. He was given a Baldwin 810CP Electric Classical Guitar, which he adored. The only problem was that after a few plays, the neck fell off. He took it to a luthier (a person who repairs string instruments), who claimed it couldn't be fixed. Instead, he offered Willie a different guitar for $750: a Martin N-20 nylon string classical. Willie agreed to take it if he installed the ceramic pickup from the Baldwin in the Martin. The luthier said, no problem and delivered the updated guitar to Willie.

Willie enjoyed it. It had the tone of an acoustic guitar but could project like an electric thanks to the ceramic pickup. Willy named it Trigger because it had the best of both worlds. And, yes, it is named after Roy Rogers horse.

Willie was on the road practically constantly from 1966 on. Shirley stayed in Tennessee and took care of Willie's kids. They never had their own children. Willie, being Willie, did what many performers do while they're on the road: he played around. Shirley was not blameless either. She had her share of affairs since she was lonely at home. Each knew what the other was up to, and while neither liked it, it was the way of life. Suddenly it all went downhill. Shirley discovered a bill from a Houston hospital for the delivery and birth of a young girl to someone called Connie Koepke while going through the mail. Willie's daughter had apparently been born, and the bill was mailed to Willie.

Shirley went through the roof. When Willie returned home the next time, there was a large quarrel, and despite their best efforts, they both knew it was pointless. Shirley left for good in late 1970. So Willie called Connie Koepke and invited her to live with him in Ridgetop, Tennessee. And she did it. In 1971, he and Shirley divorced. Willie gave the new baby girl the name Paula Carlene, and on April s0, 1972, he married her mother, Connie. She was Willie's third wife, and they were married for sixteen years, until 1988.

I must recall the huge fire of 1970. Connie was home alone just before Christmas when she discovered the house was on fire. She began calling individuals, including Willie. Willie fled when the fire department arrived. Despite the firemen's orders, he dashed into the home and saved the two most essential things to him (because everyone else had fled). He hauled out Trigger and a large bag of Columbian Gold marijuana. It's good to know Willie prioritized correctly. Anybody who knows Willie is aware of Trigger's condition. The large hole at the front of the instrument is visible. The damage has accumulated over time, and I've always wondered how it happened. The truth is that Trigger is a classical guitar and was not designed to be played with a pick, much less a metal pick, as Willie does. Beating on the strings has created a hole in the guitar that has grown with time. Willie claims to have had it repaired and reinforced several times, but he still plays Trigger and, I guess, will till the day he dies. The Willie Nelson sound is largely due to Trigger.

Willie needed a place to live now that the house in Ridgetop was gone. Fortunately, no one was injured, but many of his belongings were destroyed. Willie discovered that he could rent a house just outside of San Antonio, Texas. He was fond of Texas. He did the most of his work in Texas. Texas felt familiar. It would be nice to return to Texas. That is exactly what they did. Joe and Connie, as well as the children and other folks who appeared to always stay with the Nelsons, packed up what little they had left and relocated to Texas.

They settled at the Lost Valley Dude Ranch in Bandera, Texas, just west of San Antonio. Bandera, Texas Hill Country, was known as "The Cowboy Capital of the World." Willie could not be happier. They were only supposed to stay there until his house in Ridgetop, Tennessee could be repaired, so they had to consider it a temporary situation.

Willie had a fantastic time penning music in Texas. While living at the Dude Ranch, he wrote some amazing songs, some of which are included in Yecterday'c Wine. Willie's CD Yecterday'c Wine has some of his best material, although it was not commercially successful. The record was intended to be played in its entirety, something no radio station would do. Willie and RCA Records were on the verge of bankruptcy.

Willie finished three additional albums for RCA, Willie Nelson and Family (#4s), The Words Don't Suit the Picture (didn't chart), and The Willie Way (#s4). His contract with RCA expired at that point, and the two split ways. The only thing I can say about these three albums is that The Words Don't Suit the Picture has the initial recording of "Good Hearted Lady," which Willie later recorded with Waylon Jennings and took to number one. In 1972, it wasn't even released as a single.

Waylon Jennings wrote the majority of "Good Hearted Lady." Waylon was inspired by a newspaper article mentioning Ike and Tina Turner and their issues. He believed the statement in the article about Tina Turner being "a good-hearted woman loving' two-timing men" was a perfect basis for a song. He labored on the song till he realized he was missing one line and couldn't come up with it.

During a poker session with Waylon, Willie, and several buddies, Waylon expressed his concern to Willie. Willie filled in for the missing line. The line begins, "With teardrops and laughter..." Waylon stated, and the song was finished. Willie was given co-writer rank for the song because of just one line. Waylon recorded the song himself in 1972, and it became his third number-one smash. Later, in 1975, he re-mixed the song, adding Willie singing along with him, as well as audience noises to give the impression that it was a live performance, and re-released it. This time, it topped the country chart and reached number 25 on the Billboard Hot 100, the pop chart. The song won Single of the Year at the 1976 CMA Awards and helped both Waylon and Willie become superstars.

The house in Ridgetop was rebuilt and ready to move into after a few months in Texas. So Willie and his family returned to Tennessee to begin a new life. Willie was on his last RCA album, and he didn't like Tennessee all that much. When his contract expired, he and his family relocated from Tennessee to Texas.

Reunion in Dripping Springs

Willie took part in a concert shortly after returning to Texas that would determine his future and the futures of numerous other musicians. It would also establish Austin, Texas as the state's music capital. It was known as the Dripping Springs Reunion, and it took place outside of Austin for three days in March 1972. Its original goal was to recreate the popularity of Woodstock in New York State in 1969, but solely for country music. The first day included mostly bluegrass, while the second day featured the great artists of country music in 1972, such as Tex Ritter, Hank Snow, and Sonny James. The third day was on Sunday, and it featured Willie and other newcomers to country music. The third day featured Willie, Waylon Jennings, and Kris Kristofferson, as well as Buck and Bonnie Owens and Tom T Hall. These were all members of the country's new generation.

The Dripping Springs Reunion was notable because it brought together three people who would become friends for years and record together many times, Willie, Waylon Jennings, and Kris Kristofferson. It also established a precedent, at least in Willie's opinion, for future activities such as the yearly picnic he would throw in subsequent years.

Willie hired the man who would be his manager for the next five years or so in 1972. Reshen, Neil. Reshen was significantly responsible for Willie signing with Atlantic and other labels.

Willie was residing in Austin by 1972, playing every night at a bar or club and having a good time. He wasn't making much money, but it had never been about money for him. In 1972, Atlantic Records approached him. They were attempting to establish a country music section (which they had never done before) and wanted Willie to be a part of it. He replied OK because he was done with RCA and recorded two initial albums for Atlantic, one secular and one gospel. The gospel record was titled The Troublemaker, but Atlantic never published it. They were new to country music and didn't think the record was appropriate for the label. It would be issued on the Columbia label four years later. Shotgun Willie, a secular record, was released.

Willie's nickname, and it signaled a shift in Willie's musical style. The title song, "Shotgun Willie," was composed on a box of sanitary napkins in a bathroom. Willie wrote whenever he felt inspired. Shotgun Willie, published by Atlantic in June of 1977, is claimed to be one of the first of the so-called "outlaw albums" for which Willie, Waylon, and Johnny Cash became famous. The album performed poorly, peaking at number 41, but it signaled a new approach for Willie.

The origins of the nickname "Shotgun Willie" are fascinating. Willie was informed by one of his daughters that another of his children, Lana (his first child, a daughter of Willie and Martha), was being abused by her husband Steve Warren. Initially, Willie went to Warren's residence and battled briefly with him, warning him that if he touched his daughter, he would be in big trouble. Willie went home, and not long after, Warren and his cronies arrived, firing .22 guns at Willie's house. Willie fired back, and they fled, only to return shortly thereafter. Willie pulled out an M1 Garand weapon, which is formidable artillery, and shot Warren's truck with it, effectively ending the rivalry. Willie was known as "Shotgun Willie" from then on, at least until another nickname was coined. It's interesting that the cops never showed up during the whole thing.

Willie bought a 44-acre ranch west of Austin, Texas, using the money he earned from signing with Atlantic and relocated his family there. He was thinking about the Dripping Springs Reunion in June of the 1970s when he told a friend, "I think we should have a picnic," and he wanted it to be on July 4th. It was less than a month away, so everyone was scrambling to contact friends and others who might want to visit the ranch.

They put up a display that rivaled anything anyone had ever seen in one month. They also convinced the performers to work for a share of the gate. Tickets were $5.50 in advance and $6 at the door. Waylon Jennings and his wife Rita Coolidge, Sammi Smith, Billy Joe Shaver, John Prine, Lee Clayton, Leon Russell (who wasn't really country, but Willie liked him anyhow,) Tom T Hall, Hank Cochran, Johnny Bush, Ray Price, Loretta Lynn, Ernest Tubb were also on the bill. Charlie Rich and Larry Gatlin. (Whew) There were a few more, but that's the primary one. Bob Dylan was supposed to appear, but he never did. That rumor most likely did not come true.

Any effect on ticket sales? The picnic grew so large in such a short period of time that it had to be held at the Hurlbut Ranch near Dripping Springs, the same location as the reunion that prompted the whole thing. An estimated 40,000 people attended. It felt like Woodstock all over again.

The picnic became an annual tradition. The following year, 80,000 people attended, and the numbers only grew from there. It was held in Tulsa, Oklahoma in 1977, and in Kansas City, Missouri in 1978. Austin was the most popular destination in the 1980s. The event was held in Luckenbach, Texas in the 1990s. Billy Bob's Texas at the Fort Worth Stockyards was a popular hangout in the 2000s. (Check out the e-cover.) book's

He released one more album for Atlantic, Phases and Stages, which performed slightly better than Shotgun Willie, peaking at number four. It was a concept album about a man and a woman's breakup. The album was unique in that one side featured all songs from the perspective of the male, while the other side contained all songs from the perspective of the woman. In writing the songs, Willie was inspired by his first marriage to Martha. Phases and Stages was released in March 1974, and the album's song "Bloody Mary Morning" reached number seventeen on the country chart.

Willie teamed up with another country artist, Tracy Nelson (no related), who had had limited success up to that point. They recorded "After the Fire Is Gone," a duet performed by Conway Twitty and Loretta Lynn a few years before. The original version had reached number one for Twitty and Lynn, but Nelson's rendition only reached number seventeen. Willie has not recorded a duet since 1961, when he sang with Shirley Collins. In 1974, the song earned them a Grammy nomination for Best Country Duo.

Atlantic Nashville discovered after one and a half years of attempting that it was not producing the necessary profits. They closed the label on September 7, 1974, leaving Willie without a label once more. It wasn't for long. His pal Waylon Jennings recorded for Columbia, and the label's executives kept their finger on the pulse of the industry. They knew Willie was leaving Atlantic, so they approached him and asked him if he wanted to join Columbia. He did, and he was quickly signed. The cherry on top was that Columbia granted Willie complete creative control over the music he would make. That meant Willie could finally record whatever he wanted without having to answer to anyone.

Stranger with a Red Head

Willie had a new label, which meant he needed to create a new album. Willie and Connie were driving back to Austin from Steamboat Springs, Colorado, when Willie said that he needed an album. Connie suggested he start with The Story of the Red Headed Stranger, which Willie used to play on his radio show, and they brainstormed ideas for further songs from there. The album would be a concept album, with all of the songs centered around the title song. It was known as Red Headed Stranger. It came out in May of 1975. It was slightly over ss minutes long at its longest. A rather brief album.

Willie was offered $60,000 to make the album, but he only spent $4,000 on it. He kept the rest. One explanation for the low price was the album's small number of musicians. There are a total of eight players mentioned. Willie is the sole vocalist; no support vocalists are present. As a result, the record has a highly soulful vibe. You feel as if you're in the room with him as he plays. It's really private. That's what the Columbia executives didn't comprehend. The majority of the label's employees despised the record. They'd never heard anything like it before. Columbia was unsure whether to distribute it, but several people listened to it and became believers. If you listen to the album in order, it tells a tale. It portrays the story of a preacher who is on the run from the authorities after murdering his wife and her boyfriend.

Columbia wanted to release "Remember Me" as the first single, and it's a great song. It's fast-paced, and I enjoy the piano solo in the middle. Some, though, had different ideas. The people were mostly the DJs who played Willie's songs. They informed Columbia that the song "Blue Eyes Weeping in the Rain" was the greatest and should be released first.

As a result, Columbia went with the DJs, and Willie got his first number one single. Willie Nelson did not write "Blue Eyes Crying in the Rain." It was composed by Fred Rose in 1947, and Roy Acuff was the first to record it.

Willie Nelson was no stranger to the country music industry or the country music charts. He had, however, never hit it big. He required

something that would launch him into prominence, and "Blue Eyes" achieved just that. The song lasted two weeks at the top of the country singles chart and eighteen weeks overall. The song also crossed over and debuted on the pop chart, peaking at number 22 on the Billboard Hot 100. Willie's first pop smash, but it was far from his last. The song is ranked number s02 on Rolling Stone Magazine's list of the 500 Greatest Songs of All Time.

The album Red Headed Stranger performed similarly well. It also debuted at the top of the album chart. The album was ranked number 18 on Rolling Stone Magazine's list of the 500 Greatest Albums of All Time. The album is ranked number one on Country Music Television's (CMT) list of the 40 Greatest Albums in Country Mucig. Willie hit a home run with Red Headed Stranger, in my opinion. By 1976, the album had sold 2 million copies, earning it double platinum status. Willie went from being an opening act to being the main attraction. "Remember Me" was released as the second single and peaked at number two on the singles list.
Willie was back in the studio by Christmas 1975, working on his second album, The Count in Your Head. Willie wanted to make an album of all the songs that people appeared to enjoy when they were on tour. But there's not much new on the CD. Willie primarily covers classic tunes and songs by other artists. Nonetheless, the album was another number one, giving him two in a row. Columbia was overjoyed.

The album's first single, "I'd Have to Be Crazy," written by Steve Fromholz, peaked at number eleven on the charts. It was a unique thrill for Fromholz to sing along with Willie on his song. If you listen to the music, you can plainly hear Fromholz in the background around the two-minute mark. That was completely unintentional, but they left it in.

"If You've Got the Money (I've Got the Time)," the second single from The Cound in Your Mind, is an old Lefty Frizzell song from 1950. Frizzell also recorded for Columbia, which likely made obtaining rights to the song easier. In 1950, he took it to number one, and Willie did the same in 1976. It was his second number one position. The Count in Your Head was chosen the best country album of the year by Billboard Magazine.

Remember Willie's 1972 album The Troublemaker, which he made with Atlantic? Willie made a gospel album, but Atlantic didn't think it was fit for the label, so they didn't release it. Willie retained ownership of the album and chose Columbia to release The Troublemaker as his next album. Gospel doesn't normally sell well, but Willie was coming off two number one albums in a row, which gave The Troublemaker the boost it needed, and Willie got his third number one.

They charted one single from the album, "Uncloudy Day," which reached number four.

The Big Deal

Willie Nelson became a celebrity overnight. He was selling albums and everyone knew who he was. He agreed to play at Caesar's Palace in Las Vegas on a multi-million dollar contract. Willie's musical style was becoming popular. They called it Progressive Country, and several radio stations in Texas played it. They also performed with Waylon Jennings, The Allman Brothers, Poco, and Pure Prairie League in addition to Willie.

Willie had a lot of fans before, but it was absurd now. Supporters began to emerge from the shadows. They would try to get close to him by hopping the fence around his residence. They hired security, but nothing could keep them out. The crowds just kept on coming. Connie, his wife, was afraid. She couldn't live in a house that was under constant attack. The kids were in danger, and Willie was gone most of the time, so he couldn't help.

It eventually became too much. In the summer of 1976, Connie and her two daughters left Texas for Conifer, Colorado. They moved again a year later to Evergreen, Colorado, some 27 miles southeast of Denver, where they acquired 122 acres and were far enough away from the fans that they didn't mind. Willie was being pursued by the crowd, and he was still in Texas, so Connie finally felt safe. Willie stayed in Texas but came back whenever he could.

Wanted: The Outlaw was released on the RCA label on January 12, 1976. It went double platinum (2 million copies sold) and peaked at number one on the country album chart (where it remained for six weeks). It also peaked at number ten on the pop chart. Wanted: The Outlaw was the first country music album to be certified platinum, much alone double platinum, in the RIAA's history. The album was primarily a compilation of previously released songs, although it had the best of the greatest. It also included Waylon Jennings and his wife Jessi Colter, as well as Tompall Glaser.

The tracks on this album that I find noteworthy include "Good Hearted Lady," a 1972 duet between Willie and Waylon that I have already discussed.

about. Waylon Jennings also sang the song "My Heroes Have Always Been Cowboys," which Willie would take to number one four years later. The song was never released as a single by Waylon. Waylon and Jessi recorded "Suspicious Minds," an Elvis Presley song that hit number 25 on the country charts. Many different people have performed the song.

Willie has long been renowned for his marijuana use, but in 1976, he went all in. He stopped smoking normal cigarettes and only smoked marijuana. He also quit drinking heavily. Willie was a bad alcoholic, and even when he was sober, he was difficult to get along with. He discovered that marijuana mellowed him out, and he stopped punching holes in walls and kicking down doors. To be fair, Willie was a busy man. He was continually recording. He was continually performing, and it was wearing on him. The weed made everything appear to be fine.

Cocaine was also the drug of choice for most performers, including Willie and his band. Willie, on the other hand, didn't use cocaine all that much. One of his catchphrases was "Speed and cannabis don't mix," and he meant it. He was called before a federal grand jury investigating cocaine and heroin use in Texas in 1976. Willie could honestly pretend he had no idea.

Willie discovered in the summer of 1977 that his manager, Neil Reshen, had been submitting tax extensions on Willie's income for the previous five years while never filing the taxes themselves. Willie now owed back taxes for five years. To make matters worse, Reshen shipped a cocaine box from New York to Nashville addressed to Waylon Jennings. Waylon was arrested for cocaine possession after the DEA intercepted the shipment. These accusations were ultimately dropped after Reshen's assistant, Mark Rothbaum, stepped in and accepted responsibility for the narcotics.

To safeguard Willie, Rothbaum went to jail and served time. When Willie discovered that Reshen had not been paying his taxes, he sacked him and promised Rothbaum that he could have Reshen's position when he was released from prison. He employed him before going to prison and paid him the entire time he was there. Willie was a wonderful person. According to reports, the warden liked Willie Nelson, therefore Rothbaum's sentence was lowered from years to a few months.

Willie released an album of Lefty Frizzell tunes in 1977. To Lefty From Willie was recorded in 1975, but Colombia had dumped Frizzell three years before and just didn't think he was important anymore, so it sat for two years. Willie had complete artistic control over his song, therefore he opted to release it in June 1977. Willie, on the other hand, had the final laugh, as the record reached number two on the country album list and number 91 on the Billboard Hot 200, which covers all genres. "I Love You a Thousand Ways," one of the album's singles, peaked at number nine.

Waylon Jennings also recorded his smash hit "Luckenbach, Texas (Back to the Fundamentals of Love)" in 1977, which was Waylon's biggest song of his career. Nothing better epitomizes country music than "Luckenbach, Texas." Willie doesn't get label credit on the song, but in the final verse, he steps in and sings with Waylon, and everyone who heard it understood right away who was on the record. This song was virtually as important to Willie's career as it was to Waylon's.

Considering the popularity of "Luckenbach, Texas," it only made sense for them to create a duet album, which they did. That wasn't simple because they were recording for different labels, but after sitting down and ironing out the technicalities, both labels (RCA and Columbia) agreed. And I'm sure they're relieved they did it. Waylon and Willie was another number one album when it was released in January 1978. It held the top spot on the country chart for three months. The song peaked at number twelve on the Billboard Top

200. Another number one song from the album is "Mammas, Don't Let Your Kids Grow Up to Be Cowboys."

Willie had rented a condo in Malibu, California, and had relocated Connie and the girls there in 1977. They desired to be close to Waylon's children, but Waylon and Jessi lived in California. Willie was surprised and delighted to discover that he was living just beneath Booker T. Jones. You might not recall Booker T. Washington. & the M.G.s, although they had a two mainstream songs in the Sixties, one was "Green Onions," which was a number three song in 1962, and his other big hit was "Hang 'Em High," which was a number nine in 1968 (he had other minor singles). could truly groove, and he'd been a prominent figure in the music industry ever since.

Willie and Booker T. Jr. They quickly became friends and discovered that they both like traditional American music. Willie loved standards even though he played country music, so the two of them started a mission to create an album of standards. Stardust, published in April 1978, has ten songs from the American Songbook, standards that people have been listening to for years, all with a Willie Nelson twist. The album debuted at number one on the country album chart and at number s0 on the Billboard Top 200. Thus, another home run for Willie.

From the album, he also had two number one singles: "Georgia On My Mind," written by Hoagy Carmichael and Stuart Gorrell in 19s0, and "Blue Skies," penned by Irving Berlin in 1926. "All of Me," penned by Gerald Marks and Seymour Simons in 1921, was first recorded by Ruth Etting and charted at number three. Booker T. He not only produced the album, but he also plays piano and organ on several of the songs.

With four number one albums in a row, Willie Nelson was on top of the world. He was as famous as it gets in country music. President Carter brought Ctarduct to the White House for a concert two weeks following his release. Carter invited him back for a private concert in

September 1978. Willie was able to spend the night at the White House during this visit. They put him up in the Lincoln Bedroom, and later that night, just as Willie was ready to retire for the night, a buddy knocked on the door and asked if he wanted a tour of the White House. You don't say no to anything like that, so Willie went along with him.

The tour took them through the building till they arrived on the roof. They could see the Washington Monument, the Jefferson Memorial, and the Capitol from there. Willie accepted the friend's offer of a joint from his pocket. He naturally agreed. So it's the middle of the night, and Willie is smoking marijuana on the White House roof. Who else could claim to have done that? Willie Nelson is the only one. According to some reports, this occurred in 1977 rather than 1978. It doesn't matter; I'm fairly certain it occurred. In any case, it's a fantastic story.

Late in 1978, he released Willie and Family Live (#1), which included a live rendition of "Whiskey River," which peaked at number twelve.

Willie had always admired Leon Russell, but they had never collaborated. In 1979, they released One For the Road, a duet album in the style of Waylon and Willie. It lacked the star power.

Waylon and Willie were chosen since many people did not remember Russell. It did, however, yield one number one record, a rendition of Elvis Presley's "Heartbreak Hotel," and it showed that Russell and Willie bended extremely well together.

Booker T. Jerry Reed, who was doing well on his own, also joined the family. In order to capitalize on the success of To Lefty From Willie, they recorded Willie Nelson Cingc Krictoffercon, a 9-song album of all Kris Kristofferson songs that was published in October 1979. It reached number five. They had so much fun playing together that Russell joined Willie on his following tour. Willie recorded his first Christmas album, Beautiful Paper, after the tour, which was released in November 1979. It peaked at number eleven, a respectable position for a Christmas album.

Willie also began growing his empire in Texas in 1979. Willie noticed the potential of the Pedernales Country Club in Lake Travis, Texas, about s0 miles west of Austin, and put in a bid on the property. He eventually acquired the property and made it his own after some haggling. It had a golf course, a few buildings, and a lot of acreage. Willie reasoned that this would be a nice spot to bring friends and mingle, play some golf, drink, and have a good time. This is where he held his summer picnic in 1979. Over 20,000 people came. At Pedernales, Willie also established a world-class recording facility. Several of the greatest musicians of all time recorded there, as did Willie.

Electric Horseman

Willie and Connie were aboard a plane with Robert Redford in early 1979. They were awestruck, and to be honest, so was Redford. Willie and Connie were invited to Redford's ranch in Utah. While they were horseback riding, Redford asked Willie whether he had ever considered acting. Willie had not only considered it, but it was one of the primary reasons he had relocated his family to California.

Willie soon received a call from Sydney Pollack, the director/producer in charge of Redford's next film, The Electric Horseman. Willie didn't even have to audition, in my opinion. They simply cast him in the role. He acted as Robert Redford's sidekick. He portrayed Wendell Hickson, the manager of a disgraced rodeo rider named Sonny Steele, who was reduced to making morning cereal commercials. Jane Fonda also appeared in the film as Redford's love interest.

Willie's biggest contribution to the film, aside from acting, was an updated version of "My Heroes Have Always Been Cowboys," which Waylon Jennings had done for the Wanted! The Outlaws album was released in 1976. The song reached number 44 on the pop list after reaching number one on the country chart for the eighth time. The film was released in December 1979, and the song reached number one in January 1980.

The Electric Cowboys last charting song was "Midnight Rider," which was made popular by Gregg Allman of the Allman Brothers and reached number nineteen in 1974. Willie's version reached number six on the country chart, but I'm mixing apples and oranges because the charts are so different.

Willie performed so well in the film studio that he was cast in another film before The Electric Horseman was completed. Willie would play the lead in the next film, which was impressive for only his second feature. Willie and Dyan Cannon starred in the film Honeysuckle Rose. It sounds similar to Willie's own narrative. It's about a country musician with a wife and a daughter who is tempted to wander while on the road. Amy Irving, the actress, was the enticement. And there are reports that Willie acted on his feelings even when he wasn't on set. Does this sound familiar? Willie claimed he didn't even have to perform. It just felt right. I understand why. The picture eventually grossed over $18 million. I'm not sure how much it cost to produce, but I'm sure they earned a profit.

The best thing to come out of Honeysuckle Rose were the two number one songs on the soundtrack. Willie's first hit was "On the Road Again," which became his hallmark song. For those who aren't Willie Nelson diehards, this is perhaps his most recognizable song. It was his eleventh number one hit on the country charts. It also charted at twenty on the pop chart and seven on the Adult Contemporary chart. It was nominated for an Academy Award for Best Song, but it was defeated by "Fame" from the film of the same name. Best Country Cong earned a Grammy Award a year later. Rolling Stone Magazine named "On the Road Again " 471st among the 500 Greatest Songs of All Time. It was inducted into the Grammy Hall of Fame in 2011.

"On the Road Again" was so influential that when Honeysuckle Roce debuted on television years later, it was titled On the Road Again. It's available under both titles.

Willie also wrote "Angel Flying Too Near to the Ground," the other song on Honeysuckle Rose. It was his eighth number one single, and the song is said to be about Willie's friend and Hell's Angel Charlie "Magoo " Tinsley. That rumor has never been confirmed or disputed by Willie. Willie had employed the Hell's Angels to handle security at his concerts when he was first starting out, so he was pals with numerous of them. Others say Willie wrote the song in memory of his wife, Connie.

Willie's life was not all roses and sunshine. With all of the excellent things going on, there were two difficult things to deal with. Willie lost his father, Ira Doyle Nelson, to lung cancer in 1978, and about a year later, Nancy Wilson, Mama, who had cared for him while he was younger, died. Willie gained some perspective as a result of his losses, and he attempted to clean up his act a little. That didn't last long.

Always in my thoughts

Honeysuckle Rose was number one, followed by Somewhere Over the Rainbow, which was also number one, and then Always On My Thoughts, which was, you got it, number one. Somewhere Over the Rainbow, released in February 1981, was a return to traditional fare in the style of Stardust. It generated two songs, "Mona Lisa" (#11), composed by Ray Evans and Jay Livingston for the film Captain Carey and first sung by Nat "King" Cole in 1950. "I'm Gonna Sit Right Down and Write Myself a Letter" (#26), composed by Fred E Ahlert and Joe Young, dates from 19s5. It was featured in the Broadway production of Ain't Misbehavin'. Billy Williams recorded the version I prefer in 1957. You may watch it on YouTube. (Yeah, yea.)

Willie's album Always On My Thoughts, published in February 1982, has to be one of his best. It was Billboard's number one album of the year and spent 25 weeks on the chart. That's nearly five years. It also spent 99 weeks at the top of Billboard's Top 200 chart, peaking at number two. Willie appears to be moving away from recording his own music. He wrote only two songs for the album, "Permanently Lonely" and "The Party's Over," both of which were composed in the 1950s. Willie subsequently explained that he wasn't composing as much in the Eighties because he needed to eat. Writing was a means of making money. He'd gotten to the stage in his profession where he didn't have to worry about putting food on the table. So he could take it easy on the writing.

Willie was in the middle of recording what is likely his other most famous album when he came across "Always On My Mind." He was in the studio with Merle Haggard recording the album Pancho and Lefty when someone approached Merle and showed him the song. Merle turned it down because it didn't feel like a Merle Haggard tune. Willie liked the song and recorded it after the guy played it to him. It went on to become one of Willie Nelson's best hits. Willie has often speculated on what would have happened if Merle Haggard had accepted the tune.

Willie Nelson did not write "Always On My Mind." Johnny Christopher, Mark James, and Wayne Carson wrote it in 1972 and it was first sung by Gwen McCrae (as "You Were Always On My Thoughts") and then by Brenda Lee. Brenda Lee peaked at number 45 on the country charts. Several artists (over s00) have covered it, including Elvis Presley (never charted, it was the reverse side of "Separate Ways") and the Pet Shop Boys. Willie's rendition, on the other hand, is by far the best-selling and most popular. And Willie's rendition dominated the charts, staying at number one for two weeks. It was on the country chart for a total of 21 weeks. It also made it to the pop charts, where it peaked at number five.

The song received three Grammy Awards in February of the 1980s: Cong of the Year, Best Country Cong, and Willie himself won Best

Male Country Vocal Performance. The song was named 1982 Cong of the Year and 198S Cong of the Year at the Country Music Awards (CMAs). The Cong of the Year Award belongs to the writer, but it might not have happened without Willie. In 1982, Willie was named Cingle of the Year and Album of the Year. Do you realize the impact of just one song? Willie was unquestionably the world's ruler (at least the country world.)

While "Always on My Mind" is by far the most powerful and successful song on the album, it would be remiss not to highlight the album's other songs. The Everly Brothers first performed "Let It Be Me" in its current form in 1960. Willie finished second. The third single from the album, "Last Thing I Needed First Thing This Morning," written by Gary P Nunn and Donna Farar, reached number two.

Let's return to Pancho and Lefty. They recorded 2s tracks during the recording and still didn't feel like they had the song that would characterize the album. Although the song had not yet been discovered, the names Pancho & Lefty had not yet been mentioned, but they were soon. Townes Van Zandt wrote the song in 1972 and it was recorded by him and Emmylou Harris. Lana, Willie's daughter, heard the Emmy Lou Harris version one night and realized it was just what Willie and Merle were seeking for. She called Daddy and informed him he had one more song to record. "Pancho & Lefty " was placed on the album and became its title.

Pancho & Lefty debuted in January of the 1980s and quickly rose to the top of the charts. This album embodies the precise meaning of "outlaw country." Early vinyl pressings misspelled Pancho as Poncho, but this was swiftly remedied. If you have one of those earlier LPs with the misspelling, I'm sure it's worth a lot.

The song is about a Mexican bandit named Lefty and his companion. Pancho is based on the Mexican criminal Pancho Villa somewhat loosely. In the song, Lefty betrays Pancho, and Pancho is hanged, although in reality, Pancho Villa was slain. Pancho Villa did, in fact, have a comrade whose name translates to Lefty in Spanish. What's strange is that Townes Van Zandt was unaware of any of this when he composed the song. Townes stated that he did not create the song about Pancho Villa, but after learning of the many coincidences between the song and the guy, he concluded that the music must have come to him from another source. "That just happened out of nowhere," he explained.

I'll never forget a song that came out about this time. Willie and Waylon Jennings performed a duet on "Just to Please You," which was released in 1982. Waylon penned this song with Don Bowman in the 1960s. Waylon was just starting out in the business. He used it as the title tune for his 1968 album Just to Satisfy You. The song didn't do well until he teamed up with Willie and recorded it as a duet. It was number one for two weeks.

Willie released the album City of New Orleans in 1984, which went to number one, and the title tune, "City of New Orleans," also went to number one. Steve Goodman, an American folk singer and songwriter, wrote this tune. Arlo Guthrie recorded the song in 1972, and it has since become an American classic. Goodman was afflicted with leukemia when he was younger and lived only six years before dying in 1984. In 1985, he received a Grammy posthumously for the song. Willie's rendition is, in my opinion, one of the best.

"To All the Girls I've Ever Known"

Julio Iglesias was one of the most unexpected artists to record at Pedernales Studio. Willie first heard his music when his wife, Connie, purchased one of his albums. Willie felt they would sound excellent together since he liked his voice. He reached out to Iglesias through an intermediary, and Iglesias said he had a song for Willie. Hal David and Albert Hammond wrote "To All the Ladies I've Known Before" for Hammond's album 99 Miles From L.A. in 1975. Bobby Vinton also recorded it, and Julio got aware of it in 1984. When he learned that Willie wanted to record a duet of the song, he agreed, and the two met at Pedernales and cut the song in three takes.

"To All the Girls I've Known Before," which was released in April 1984, raced to the top of the charts. It reached number five on the pop charts (albeit it was Willie's last pop chart appearance) and introduced America to a new vocalist, Julio Iglesias, from Madrid, who was well recognized in most areas of the world but unknown in America. That is no longer the case. Even though the song was about as far from country as you can get, it reached number one on the country chart and earned Best Duo of the Year at that year's CMA Awards. Willie was fluttering his wings.

Willie enjoyed duets. He attempted to find someone to sing with as often as he could. Half Nelson was released in 1985, but before that, they released his duet with Julio Iglesias and "Seven Spanish Angels," a duet with Ray Charles, in November of 1984. You can't get much more different than Julio Iglesias and Ray Charles, but Willie sang with each of them and they both sounded fantastic. Willie and Ray Charles became close friends while recording. Ray, according to Willie, enjoyed playing chess with him. As Willie insisted on light, he discovered that all of the pieces were the same hue. Ray always defeated him.

Willie had another number one with "Seven Spanish Angels," and while Ray Charles had some success with country music (he had eight songs on the country chart), this one was his best-selling and charted the highest. Half Nelson also includes duets with Leon Russell, George Jones, Hank Williams, and Neil Young. I remember buying the album in the 1980s and enjoying it to pieces. (It's still in my possession.)

Willie was on the cover of Life Magazine in August of the 1980s, alongside his wife and two daughters. They appeared to be a happy family, but things were not going well at home. Willie had never recovered from his affair with Amy Irving when they worked together on the film Honeysuckle Roce. Willie had informed his wife that he had broken up with Irving when the truth was quite the opposite. Willie was still pining for Irving and working hard to have her back in his life.

The picnics were held year after year, with some being more successful than others. They were almost rained out in 1985, but fifteen thousand people still paid to stand in the rain and listen to music. Picnics weren't as popular as they used to be, owing to Willie's presence everywhere. He was releasing at least two albums every year and performing everywhere. Willie could be seen pretty much whenever they wanted. Why should I stand in the rain to see him? The Highwaymen were one of the bands that performed at the 1985 picnic.

The Roadrunners

Some of you may be familiar with the Traveling Wilburys, a 1980s pop supergroup composed of Roy Orbison, Bob Dylan, Tom Petty, Jeff Lynne, and George Harrison. You may read about them in the Legends of Rock and Roll - Roy Orbicon series, as well as the same series on Bob Dylan and George Harrison. Maybe I'll write novels about the two remaining members one day.

In any case, country music had its own supergroup in the 1980s. They were known as The Highwaymen, and they consisted of Johnny Cash, Kris Kristofferson, Willie Nelson, and Waylon Jennings. Johnny Cash has been written as a Legend of Country Music book, and you are currently in the middle of Willie Nelson. I'm almost certain there will be novels written about the other two.

Johnny Cash was scheduled to perform a Christmas special in Montreux, Switzerland, for ABC Television. The network informed him he could play with anybody he wanted. He went with Kris, Willie, and Waylon. So they all came to Switzerland to perform the show. According to Johnny, you received four for the price of one. They had so much fun that they decided to stay together and record an album.

Waylon Jennings was questioned by a reporter why the special was shot in Montreux. "Well, that's where Jesus was born, isn't it?" Waylon replied, looking at him. " Waylon was always cracking jokes. For approximately ten years, the four of them were together on and off. They launched their first album, The Highwaymen, in 1985 and had a number one success with the title song from that album.
Willie sings of being a highwayman, Kris of being a sailor, Waylon of being a dam builder, and Johnny of flying a starship. They all die at the end of their separate verses of the song, yet they will return and will always be present. This is a fantastic tune. If you haven't heard it in a while, check it out on YouTube or dig out an old album.

The Highwaymen released two more albums, Highwaymen 2 in the 1990s and Highwaymen - The Road Goes On in 1995 on Forever. They were all good, but none of them had the same success or impact as the first album.

Willie appeared in the 1986 film Red Headed Stranger, which was based on his earlier record of the same name. Robert Redford held the rights to the film and was preparing to star in it, but Willie bought it from him, and so Willie got to play the lead. The film, like the song, is about a disgraced Reverend who murders his wife for having an affair with another man. He spends the entire film striving to find redemption. The film premiered at the Denver International Film Festival in October 1985, however it garnered mixed reviews. Some people thought it was boring. According to the comments on imdb.com, the majority of those who saw the film loved it.

Willie recorded The Promiseland, which went to number one in 1986. David Lynn Jones wrote the album's first single, "Living in the Promiseland," which was released in February 1986 and hit number one. Willie's twelfth number one hit.

Farm Assistance

Live Aid was a concert held in July 1985 at Wembley Stadium in London, England. It was the first of its type, but it was far from the last. The goal of Live Aid was to bring together as many performers as possible to perform a benefit performance for Ethiopia's present famine. Millions of people were dying in Ethiopia, and Live Aid promoter Bob Geldof felt something should be done about it. According to reports, the benefit raised between £40 and £50 million. Over time, that figure has climbed to more than £150 million.

During the performance, one of the artists, Bob Dylan, said on the microphone that someone should do something like this to help the American farmer who was struggling due to mortgage debt. As Willie heard the remark, he thought to himself, "Why not? " As a result, Farm Aid was founded. Willie was not the only one who was involved. He enlisted the assistance of John Mellencamp and Neil Young, and Farm Aid was held on September 22, 1985. The inaugural Farm Aid lasted fourteen hours and was hosted at the University of Illinois' Memorial Stadium in Champaign, Illinois. Almost 80,000 people attended the concert to see Willie, Mellencamp, Young, Bob Dylan, Billy Joel, and others. The governor of Illinois was also present.

They raised almost $9 million that day, but Farm Aid has survived. As far as I know, it has taken place every year since (right up to 2016, when it was held on September 11). The only years they haven't attended are 1988 and 1991. Farm Aid formed an organization and was partly responsible for the Agriculture Credit Act of 1987, which Congress adopted as a result of Farm Aid pressure. This saved many farmers from foreclosure. Willie continues to serve on the Farm Aid Board of Directors.

One reason Farm Aid was missed in 1988 could have been because Willie was busy getting divorced. Willie collaborated with Kris Kristofferson and Johnny Cash (basically the complete Highwaymen) on a version of the film Ctagegoagh in 1986. The original, from 1939, starred John Wayne. Although it made money, the film was not a huge success. The mention of Ctagegoagh would be insignificant until Willie met Ann Marie DeAngelo, a makeup artist, on the set of the film. Willie and Ann Marie got along great. She was just his type. What could a man possibly do? His wife was at home in Colorado, while he was on a movie set thousands of miles away. Men will be boys, and he and Ann Marie started dating. Connie, of course, discovered them and attempted to shut it down. Willie's wandering was nothing new to her, but this was different.

Connie confronted Willie and told him to end the affair. Willie promised but did not follow through. Connie had finally had enough. This was simply too much. She'd put up with Willie's misbehavior for sixteen years, and she'd had enough. They had divorced by 1988. Willie married Ann Marie DeAngelo on September 16, 1991, and the couple is still married today. Maybe Willie got it right this time. He has two sons with Ann in the years between Connie and Ann, Lukas Autry (born December 25, 1989 and named after Gene Autry) and Jacob Micah (born May 24, 1990 and named for Sheriff Micah in television's The Rifleman.)

On December 25, 1991, three months after the wedding, they discovered Billy Nelson, Willie's kid with his first wife, Martha, hanged in a cabin in a Nashville suburb. Billie Nelson was born Willie Hugh Nelson, Jr. He spent his entire life attempting to escape his renowned father's shadow, but he was never successful. He struggled with drug addiction and, like his father, tax issues. Willie claimed that he was never happy. The cause of death was determined to be suicide. Billy was ss years old at the time of his death, and his mother had died two years before. Willie handled it as best as could be anticipated. Something I didn't know about Willie was that he supposedly believes in reincarnation, which helped to relieve the pain of his passing.

Willie kept recording despite the tragedy and the tax troubles. During the decade of the 1980s, he released fourteen solo albums and thirteen collaborations with other artists. Pangho and Lefty were arguably the most popular of these. In 1989, he recorded A Horce Named Mucig, which was released in July and reached number two. It featured his fourteenth number one single, "Nothing I Can Do About It Now," which was released in April. Beth Nielsen Chapman created it. The only other single from the album to chart was "There You Are" (#8).

Tax Issues

Willie's financial world imploded around him in 1991. Willie was never concerned about money or taxes. He had folks who were concerned about those things. But, those individuals were not performing their duties. Every year between 1974 and 1977, tax extensions were submitted, but no taxes were paid. This carried on for years, with Willie falling more behind in his payments to the government. You've probably heard of his business connections with Price Waterhouse. I read that they weren't paying his taxes, but that's not fully correct. Price Waterhouse agreed with Willie that they would invest a big portion of his money in tax shelters so that he would not have to pay taxes on it. However, that only works when the tax shelter is profitable. Willie was worse off when all of his investments collapsed.

The IRS had had enough by 1990. Willie was playing golf on his private course in Pedernales one day when he was suddenly encircled by a dozen federal investigators. He was arrested and taken away. The authorities simply assumed that Willie was concealing a large sum of money somewhere on his property, so they executed a search warrant and searched his safes and wherever else they could, but they found nothing. Willie didn't have a lot of liquid assets. As a result, they confiscated his home and padlocked the entrance, preventing him from using it. Next they placed the house up for auction, hoping to obtain a few million dollars for it, but that also backfired. Just local farmers attended the auction, and the farmers adored Willie. For years, he had been preaching their cause. The IRS received exactly one bid on the residence, for the actual worth of $2,840.

Willie had to have known this was going to happen. He trusted people with his cash, yet he had to know something wasn't right. I don't think he gave a damn. He was confident that everything would be fine. It was discovered that he owed the IRS $s2 million. That was negotiated down to $16 million, then to $6 million. He had excellent legal counsel. He released an album called The IRC Tapec: Who'll Purchase My Memories and announced that all proceeds will be used to settle his tax burden. The IRS did, in fact, play a role in the album's recording, a first in the IRS's history. Willie had to come up with the balance of the money when the album made roughly $s.6 million.

He owes $6 million. The album is one of his most melancholy. It featured 25 songs performed solely by Willie and his guitar.

Willie Nelson is awesome since none of this affected him. He was the personification of the "What? Should I be concerned? "personification" is a formalized phrase. He was an everlasting optimist who believed that everything will work out in the end. The IRS sold his house, golf course, fishing camp, recording studio, and even his gold recordings. The man who bought Willie's grand piano returned it to him, but I'm not sure where he kept it.

Willie's debt to the government was ultimately settled in the 199s, and he could move on with his life. What's remarkable about this entire situation is that Willie could have saved himself a lot of money simply by declaring bankruptcy. But he refused to do it. He was an honest person who realized he had gotten himself into difficulty and was determined to get out of it the right way, not by taking a shortcut. Willie Nelson deserves a lot of credit for it.

What was happening did not take precedence above music. In 1991, he reunited with Waylon Jennings once more to record Clean Shirt. It was released on July 2, 1991, and peaked at number 29 on the country album chart. There were no notable hits from the album. I saw that both of these artists had progressed to the point in their careers where they could be identified by only one name. On the pop side, we had Madonna and Cher, and now we have Waylon and Willie from the country. Clean Chirt's CD cover simply stated "Waylon and Willie," and everyone knew who that meant.

Missouri, Branson

Willie agreed to perform at the Mel Tillis Theater in Branson, Missouri in May 1992. Willie, on the other hand, despised it from the start. Branson was designed so that the audience came to the performance rather than the performer going to the audience. Willie was used to being on the go and despised being stuck in one spot. It didn't take long for him to want to leave.

Willie was inducted into the Country Music Hall of Fame in the 1990s, which is a rare award. Willie was honored, but not overjoyed. But he accepted it with grace. He needed a successful record. His previous two albums had not charted at all, and he had last entered the Top 10 in 1989.

Across the Borderline, released on March 2, 1999, was expected to be the next big album, and while it fared well, it wasn't the monster Willie had hoped for. All of the duets on this CD are fantastic. Willie collaborated on songs with Paul Simon, Bonnie Raitt, and Bob Dylan. Despite this, the record only reached number fifteen on the country album list. It did, however, chart on the pop chart, which was a positive thing. Willie's career was obviously slowing down.

When your career begins to falter, the only thing you do is switch labels. You try to get new eyes and minds on the problem. His contract with Columbia/Sony expired, and they chose not to renew it. Willie was unconcerned. He released music on a variety of labels. Over the rest of the 1990s, he released Moonlight Becomes You (#s7) on Justice Records, Healing Hands of Time (#17) on Capitol Records, and Cix Hours at Pedernales (did not ghart) on a small label named Step One Records.

Willie was requested to perform "Amazing Grace" at Bill and Melinda Gates' wedding on January 1, 1994. For the song, Gates paid him $1 million. That is slightly higher than the minimum wage.

As the decade comes to a close, there are only two albums that made a substantial impact on the charts. Willie appears to be returning to his origins, since he is now writing the majority of the songs on the CDs. Cpirit (#20), released in 1996 on the Island Record label, is a very beautiful album that yielded no singles. Willie wrote the entire thing. It's straightforward, with only two guitars, a piano, and a violin. Willie's sister Bobbie, who has accompanied him for the majority of his career, played the piano. It has a panish/classical vibe about it. Teatro (#17), released in 1998 on Island Records, performed slightly better than Cpirit. Willie authored ten of the album's fourteen tunes. Teatro was recorded in Oxnard, California, in an ancient movie theater. I'm not sure why, unless the acoustics were suitable for what Willie wanted to produce.

Between Spirit and Teatro, there was a gospel record, and Willie's voice is ideal for gospel music. How Awesome Thou Art did not chart, yet it is a terrific CD if you enjoy gospel music.

Willie finished the century with Night and Day, an instrumental album published in 1999 that features eleven songs, most of which are classics, a couple of which he had previously performed, and some which were new to him. Trigger was used as a jazz guitar by him. The record did not chart, yet it was a work of art.

The Twentieth Century

Willie just kept doing what he did best after the turn of the century. He continued to release albums, and while singles were still created, he did not frequently reach the Top 40. Willie Nelson's first Top 40 hit in the twenty-first century was "Mendocino County Line" (#22), a duet with Lee Ann Womack. Bernie Taupin, Elton John's songwriter, collaborated on the song. It was released in 2002 as a single from the album The Great Divide. Willie's highest ranking album since A Horce Called Mucig reached number two in 1989, it peaked at number five on the country album list.

The Great Divide delivered a second notable single, but it fell short of the Top 40 at 41. "Maria, (Shut Up and Kiss Me)" was another duet, this time with Matchbox Twenty's Rob Thomas. Thomas scored a tremendous hit on the music charts with Carlos Santana's song "Smooth." In reality, "Smooth" was the twentieth century's final number one pop hit. But, Thomas and Willie were unable to replicate their previous success.

Willie then collaborated with Toby Keith on "Beer For My Horses," which brought him back to the top with a number one. It was launched on April 7, 200s and spent six weeks at the top of the charts. Willie's first number one on the country chart (or any chart, for that matter) since 1989's "Nothing I Can Do About It Now," and his twenty-third overall. It also established Willie as the oldest individual in country music to reach number one. In the 200s, he was seventy. Based on the song, they created a film of the same name in 2008. It starred Toby Keith and Rodney Carrington, with Willie playing a minor role. The film did poorly and is considered a flop. It's made money throughout the years, so they may have recovered their production costs.

I can't talk about Toby Keith without discussing "I'll Never Smoke Pot with Willie Again," a great song about marijuana smoking with Willie. I've seen Toby Keith perform two or three times, and this song is always on his setlist. The song was featured as a bonus track on Toby's Chick'n Y'all album, but it was never released as a single, as far as I know. You can always listen to it on YouTube.

Episode 12 of Tony Shalhoub's television sitcom Monk's first season (2002) was titled "Mr. Willie appeared in the film "Monk and the Red-Headed Stranger." He played himself and was jailed for murder, but Mr. Monk was convinced he was innocent and spent the hour proving it.

Willie maintained recording despite dwindling sales. Willie as a solo act was no longer cutting it. From this point on, the majority of his hits were collaborations with others. You Don't Know Me: The Congc of Cindy Walker was an exception to this norm. Cindy Walker was a singer-songwriter who had been active since the 1940s. She is still regarded as the best female country songwriter in the business. Willie had long liked her, and it is a compliment to him that he chose to record an entire album of music by another composer.

Cindy had hesitantly sent Willie a demo recording of a song she thought he may like. After he heard it, he wanted to make an entire album out of her songs. So they approached Cindy, and she sent Willie 62 tunes. He and his team chose one of them to be the album. You Don't Know Me: The Congc of Cindy Walker debuted at number 24 on the country album chart on March 16, 2006. Cindy Walker died one week later, on March 2, 2006, at the age of 87.

Willie's persistent playing of the guitar for thirty years finally caught up with him in the 200s. His bandmates spotted him shaking his hand after each number, so he went to the doctor. He suffered carpal tunnel syndrome and required surgery to correct it. That took him four months off the road and out of the studio. He had been remaining after every event for years, signing autographs for the crowd. He'd stay until everyone had an autograph. That could take hours at times. Everything came to a halt. Willie couldn't take it any longer.

Ray Charles, a friend of his, died in June 2004. Willie came to see him before he died, and he was grateful. Willie Nelson sang "Georgia On My Mind" at his funeral, a song that reached number one for both Willie Nelson and Ray Charles.

If you go to imdb.com and search for Willie Nelson, you'll find a long list of his achievements. He has composed music for numerous television shows and has also starred in several. There are 256 soundtrack allusions, which are far too numerous to detail here. He has 49 acting credits, beginning with The Rockford Files in 1978 and continuing to the present day. My Cricket and Me is currently in post-production (2016) and is scheduled to air in 2017, indicating that he is still working to this day. Is he ever going to slow down? Who can say? "If he slowed down, he'd die," Carl Cornelius, a longtime friend and owner of a truck stop in Hill County, Texas, claimed.

Country music had evolved to the point where, in the early 2000s, you had to listen to an oldies station to hear Willie Nelson. He was no longer important. A new generation of country singers has emerged. Willie, on the other hand, kept pressing forward.
Willie's band members can now all claim AARP membership. Willie is 8 years old, and his sister, Bobby Lee, who still plays piano for the band, is 85 years old. Jody Payne, Willie's guitarist for 35 years, died in the 201s at the age of 77. Mickey Raphael, a harmonica player, is 64 years old. His drummer, Paul English, is an 8s. He had a small stroke in 2010, but he continues to play. Willie's bassist since the beginning, Bee Spears, died of exposure in 2011. He was 62. Randall "Poodie" Locke, Willie's stage manager for thirty years, died of a heart attack in 2009 at the age of 56.

Of course, there were others, but this was the heart of the Willie Nelson Family. Those that remain are nearing the end of their journey. When Willie eventually hangs up his hat and retires, it will be a sad day. I don't think he'll do anything on his own initiative. It will either be imposed upon him due to illness or other circumstances, or he will die. In any case, the Willie Nelson band's days are numbered.

So, quit squandering your time. If you haven't seen Willie play, track him down and attend a show. You will not be sorry. He dedicates everything he does to music and fans. He does everything for you.

Willie Nelson's Legacy

Willie Nelson is a national treasure. He has so many honors that I've put most of them further down in their own section.

In 2011, he was honored into the National Agriculture Hall of Fame in appreciation of his efforts with Farm Aid.

In the 1990s, he was inducted into the Country Music Hall of Fame.

In 1998, he earned one of the highest distinctions awarded to people in the performing arts, the Kennedy Center Honors.

Rolling Stone Magazine ranks him 88th among the 100 Greatest Singers of All Time and 77th among the 100 Greatest Guitarists.
From 1975 until 1994, a collection of Willie Nelson material was added to the Wittliff collection of Southwestern Writers. Texas State University is located in San Marcos, Texas. Lyrics, screenplays, letters, concert programs, tour itineraries, posters, articles, clippings, personal effects, promotional items, souvenirs, and papers are all included in the collection.

Willie received the Nobelity Project's "Feed the Peace" award in 2014 for his efforts with Farm Aid. The Nobelity Project is a non-profit organization based in Austin, Texas that is dedicated to teaching and improving the lives of children all over the world.

Willie was admitted into the Library of Congress' National Recording Registry in 2010.

Additionally in 2010, Austin, Texas renamed Second Street Willie Nelson Boulevard and installed a statue of him in front of the new Austin City Limits studios.

Afterword

Willie Nelson celebrated his eighth birthday this year. (When I write this, it is 2016.) He is still going strong, but we all become old. There will come a time when there will be no more Willie Nelson, and the world will be a poorer place as a result.

Willie could do it all. He had two interests: music and golf. He enjoyed both and could play music with almost anyone. He'd play in the seediest bar in Austin, Texas one day and then lead the Los Angeles Philharmonic the next.

Willie has been referred to as "the Shakespeare of American music." Whether it's "On the Road Again," "Always On My Mind," or any of the hundreds of other songs he's known for, you recognize Willie Nelson's voice the moment you hear it. I was extremely fortunate to witness him live in Las Vegas. If I could, I'd go back tomorrow and see him again.

Willie Nelson is a unique American. Because of Willie Nelson, the world is a better place.

Please leave a review of "Willie Nelson" if you like it and believe others would appreciate reading about him. Thank you for taking the time to read this.

Printed in Great Britain
by Amazon